The Party Fairies

To Molly May Britton, the party girl of Perry Barr

Special thanks to
Narinder Dhami

ORCHARD BOOKS

First published in Great Britain in 2005 by Orchard Books
This edition published in 2016 by The Watts Publishing Group

5 7 9 10 8 6

© 2016 Rainbow Magic Limited.
© 2016 HIT Entertainment Limited.
Illustrations © Georgie Ripper 2005

HIT entertainment

A CIP catalogue record for this book is available from the British Library.

ISBN 978 1 40834 869 7

Printed in Great Britain

MIX
Paper from
responsible sources
FSC® C104740
FSC
www.fsc.org

The paper and board used in this book are made from wood from responsible sources

Orchard Books
An imprint of Hachette Children's Group
Part of The Watts Publishing Group Limited
Carmelite House, 50 Victoria Embankment, London EC4Y 0DZ

An Hachette UK Company
www.hachette.co.uk
www.hachettechildrens.co.uk

Polly the Party Fun Fairy

by Daisy Meadows

illustrated by Georgie Ripper

Join the **Rainbow Magic Reading Challenge!**

Read the story and collect your fairy points to climb the Reading Rainbow online. Turn to the back of the book for details!

This book is worth 5 points.

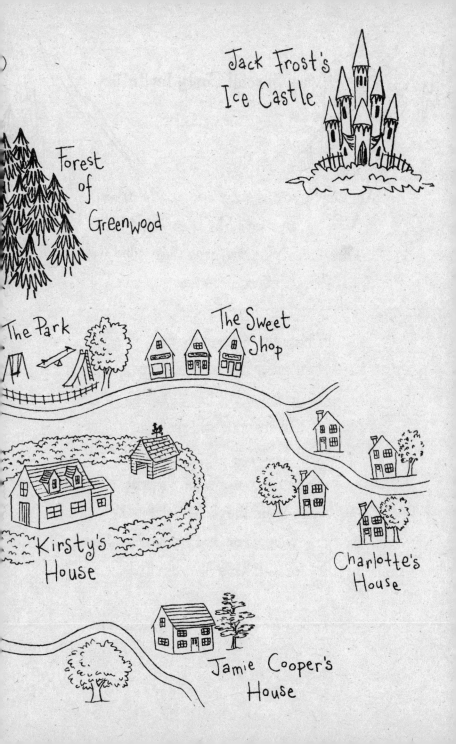

A Very Special Party Invitation

Our gracious King and gentle Queen
Are loved by fairies all.
One thousand years have they ruled well,
Through troubles great and small.

In honour of their glorious reign
A party has been planned,
To celebrate their jubilee
Throughout all Fairyland.

The party is a royal surprise,
We hope they'll be delighted.
So shine your wand and press your dress...
For you have been invited!

RSVP: HRH THE FAIRY GODMOTHER

Contents

Woodland Fun   9

Egg and Spoon Surprises   23

Polly Appears   35

Goblin Chase   45

Polly's Sparkly Secret   55

A Touch of Magic   65

Woodland Fun

"Goodbye, Mum!" Kirsty Tate called, waving from the mini-bus packed with Brownies as it pulled away from the church hall.

"Goodbye, Mrs Tate!" Rachel Walker, Kirsty's best friend, shouted, waving too.

As the mini-bus made its way through the village, Rachel turned to Kirsty.

"Isn't it great of your Brownie leader to let me come to your mini-jamboree?" she said happily.

"Well, you are staying with me this week, so I wouldn't leave you behind," laughed Kirsty. "And you're a Brownie too, even if you're not in our pack."

Rachel nodded. Both she and Kirsty were wearing their Brownie uniforms. "I'm really looking forward to this," she said eagerly. "What did you do last year?"

"We joined up with another Brownie pack — just like we're doing this time — so there were loads of us," Kirsty explained. "We played games, ran races, and there were lots of prizes. Then we had a barbecue round the camp fire." She grinned. "It was just a big party in the woods really!"

Rachel's eyes opened wide. "A party?" she gasped. "You know what that means…"

Kirsty clapped a hand to her mouth. "Oh, I didn't realise!" she said. "Of course, we'll have to be on the look-out for goblins…"

Although Kirsty and Rachel seemed just like all the other Brownies on the bus, the two girls had a special secret. They had become friends with the fairies! Now, whenever their fairy friends were in trouble, Kirsty and Rachel tried to help.

Trouble usually came in the shape of cold, spiky Jack Frost and his goblin helpers. Now Jack Frost was doing his best to ruin the secret party for the Fairy King and Queen's 1000th jubilee. The seven Party Fairies were helping with the preparations, and Jack Frost was trying to stop them by sending his goblins into the human world to spoil as many parties as they could. Then the Party Fairies would come flying to the rescue and the goblins would try to

steal their magic party bags for Jack
Frost. He intended to use the Party
Fairies' special magic to have a
fabulous party of his own.

"Yes, we'll have to keep
our eyes open," agreed
Rachel, as the mini-bus
came to a standstill
in a large woodland
clearing. There
were already lots
of Brownies milling
around. The other
pack had clearly
arrived first. "We can't
let the goblins get away
with any of the Party
Fairies' magic party bags,"
she added firmly.

13

"And we won't let them spoil our day, either," Kirsty declared, looking determined.

Mrs Talbot, Kirsty's Brownie leader, opened the door of the bus. "Here we are, girls," she said with a smile. "Go and put your bags under that big tree and we'll start with some races." A cheer went up from the Brownies on the bus as they jumped to their feet. Rachel and Kirsty were the last to clamber out. As they stepped off the bus, they both looked carefully around the clearing for any signs of goblin mayhem, but they couldn't see anything out of the ordinary.

"There are lots of places for goblins to hide here," Kirsty whispered to Rachel, as they put their bags under the spreading oak tree.

"Gather round, girls," called Mrs Talbot, who had been chatting with the other Brownie leader, Mrs Carter. "We're going to start with an obstacle race, and we need four volunteers from each pack."

Kirsty nudged Rachel. "That sounds like fun," she said. "Shall we volunteer?"

Rachel nodded, and they both put their hands up.

"Jenny and Emily," said Mrs Talbot, pointing at two girls. "Oh, and Kirsty and your friend, Rachel – you can be our team!"

Kirsty, Rachel and the other girls watched closely as Mrs Talbot showed them the course. First, they had to run along a raised plank. Then they had to scramble under a net, run along a row of upturned buckets and score a goal through a netball hoop. To finish off, all four members of the team had to jump into a rubber dinghy, and row across the wide stream that flowed along one side of the clearing.

"It looks hard," Kirsty said, nervously.

"Not as hard as trying to outwit goblins!" chuckled Rachel.

As the two teams lined up, the other
Brownies began cheering for their
teams. Mrs Carter blew her whistle, and
they were off!

Jenny ran lightly along the plank first,
followed by Rachel and then Kirsty and
Emily.

"If anyone falls off, they have to go
back to the beginning of the plank and
start again!" Mrs Talbot warned. But
both teams made it safely across.

Then they began to
wriggle under the
net. Rachel and
Kirsty's team
pulled ahead
slightly, as one of
the Brownies on the
other team got her hairclip
caught in the mesh.

By the time she was
free, Rachel and
Kirsty's team
had already
run along the
row of buckets,
and was trying
to score goals
through the
netball hoop.

"I'm hopeless at this," Emily said anxiously to Kirsty, as they watched Jenny and then Rachel score with their first shots.

"Don't worry," Kirsty replied. "Just do your best."

But after Kirsty had scored, it took poor Emily six attempts to get her goal. By then, the other team had almost caught up with them.

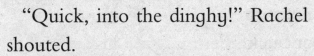

"Quick, into the dinghy!" Rachel shouted.

They all jumped in and grabbed the paddles. But as they pushed off from the bank, the other team came running over to their boat.

"Paddle harder!" shouted Jenny, as they made their way to the middle of the stream.

"They're right behind us," gasped Kirsty, glancing back.

Then, suddenly, she felt cold water seeping into her trainers. Surprised, she looked down. Water was pouring into the boat, and there was the hissing sound of air escaping as the dinghy began to deflate rapidly. It had sprung a leak!

Egg and Spoon Surprises

"Oh, no!" Kirsty shouted. "We're sinking!"

The other girls gasped.

"We'll have to bail out!" cried Rachel.

"Girls!" Mrs Talbot was standing on the bank, looking worried. "Are you all right?"

"Our dinghy's leaking!" Kirsty
yelled, as they sank even lower in
the water.

There was a shout from the
Brownies in the other boat, which
had just overtaken them. "So is ours!"

"Quickly, girls!" Mrs Carter rolled up her trousers and waded into the stream towards them. "The water's not very deep. Take your shoes and socks off, and I'll help you climb out."

The eight girls waded to the bank, dragging their now deflated dinghies

behind them. "Do you think this could be goblin mischief?" Kirsty whispered to Rachel.

"It might be," Rachel agreed with a nod.

Mrs Carter was examining one of the dinghies. "Look!" she said, pointing at the rubber. "There are some thorns stuck in there. That's what made the holes. I knew I shouldn't have put the dinghies down next to that gorse bush."

Kirsty and Rachel looked at each other.

"Maybe it was just an accident,"
Rachel said with shrug.

"Or maybe a goblin stuck those thorns
into the dinghies to make them sink!"
Kirsty pointed out.

"Oh, don't worry," Mrs Talbot was
saying, patting Mrs Carter comfortingly
on the arm. "I brought a parcel for our
pass the parcel game, and I don't even
remember where I put it! Let's have the
egg and spoon race, while I look for it."

"I'm not very good at this," Kirsty told Rachel as they queued to collect their eggs and spoons. "But it's always good fun."

"It's easier if you don't go too fast," Rachel laughed, "and keep your eye on your egg."

This time all the Brownies took part in the race. Mrs Carter blew the whistle, and they all set off, trying hard not to drop the eggs.

Rachel had a steady hand, so she was soon in the lead, but Kirsty was near the back. Suddenly, Emily rushed past her, trying to catch up with the leaders. Her hand wobbled and her egg fell and smashed on the ground. Immediately, a horrible smell filled the air.

"Ugh!" Emily shrieked, holding her nose. "My egg's rotten!"

"Yuk!" Kirsty exclaimed, covering her nose with her hand. She glanced down at her own egg to check it was steady, but then she noticed something very strange – her egg was beginning to crack.

Kirsty stopped in her tracks and another Brownie almost bumped into her. She stared at the egg as it cracked wide open. The two halves of the shell fell away, leaving a fluffy yellow chick sitting on Kirsty's spoon. It gave a little cheep. "My egg's hatched!" Kirsty gasped in amazement.

The race was forgotten
as the other
Brownies crowded
round to look at
the sweet little
chick. But just
then there was
the sound of
more eggs
cracking. Soon five
other surprised Brownies
had chicks sitting on their spoons
instead of eggs!

The two Brownie leaders could hardly
believe their eyes.

"Well, this is very strange!" said Mrs
Carter. "I hard-boiled the eggs for this
race. I suppose they must have got
mixed up with some uncooked ones."

"Do you think the goblins could have switched the eggs?" Kirsty muttered quietly to Rachel. But before Rachel could reply, Kirsty noticed that her chick had hopped off the spoon and was wandering away. "Hey, come back!" she cried.

Quite a few of the chicks had decided to make a break for freedom. The Brownies scattered to find them, and Kirsty and Rachel followed Kirsty's chick into the trees.

"There he is," Kirsty said, pointing at the roots of a tree where the chick was pecking around in the soil. Then she looked puzzled. "What's that shimmering blue light at the bottom of the tree?"

Rachel let out a gasp of delight. "Kirsty, it must be Polly the Party Fun Fairy!" she declared.

Polly Appears

Rachel was right. As Kirsty stared at
the roots of the tree, Polly the Party
Fun Fairy fluttered up into the air,
waving her wand happily. She wore a
sparkly, blue vest, and matching
trousers with a purple belt and balloon.
Long red hair tumbled over her
shoulders in untidy, shining waves.

"I'm so glad to see you, girls!" she called in a silvery, bell-like voice, her green eyes gleaming with joy. "I was hoping you'd come and find me."

"Is everything all right?" asked Kirsty, gently picking up her chick.

Polly looked a bit sad for a moment. "Well, I've lost my party bag," she said, looking round. "I'm sure I put it down here somewhere, but I just can't seem to find it at the moment." She grinned cheekily. "The other Party Fairies say I'm always losing things!"

"Maybe a goblin has stolen it," Rachel suggested.

"No, I don't think so." Polly shook her head, not looking at all worried. "I haven't seen a single goblin anywhere about."

Kirsty and Rachel looked at each other anxiously. After what had happened at the mini-jamboree so far, they were pretty sure that there was a goblin lurking somewhere. But before they had a chance to convince Polly, they heard Jenny calling from the clearing.

"Kirsty! Rachel! Where are you? We're going to play Frisbee now!"

"You go and play," Polly said with a smile. "I'll carry on looking for my party bag."

Rachel agreed, "But Polly, do be careful. Kirsty and I think there might be a goblin close by."

"We'll come and see you again later," Kirsty promised. Cradling her chick in her hand, she and Rachel hurried back to join the others.

"Pop your chick in here, Kirsty," said Mrs Carter, indicating a large cardboard box.

"I'll take all of them to the local farm later. They have a lot of free-range chickens there, so these chicks will have a good home."

Mrs Talbot organised the Brownies into a circle, and they began throwing the Frisbee to each other. It was good fun, and Kirsty and Rachel were enjoying themselves. But at the same time they couldn't help thinking about Polly and her missing party bag. What if a goblin had got hold of it?

Suddenly, one of the Brownies tossed the Frisbee very high into the air towards Kirsty. It sailed over Kirsty's head and landed in a bush under the tree where Polly was searching for her party bag.

Kirsty raced off towards the bush. "I'll get that!" she shouted. She couldn't risk Polly being spotted by any of the other Brownies.

"I'll help you look for it," Rachel called, running after her.

Behind them, Mrs Talbot was saying, "Well, that's enough Frisbee for now, girls. Let's have some juice and biscuits."

"Phew, that was close," Kirsty whispered, as she and Rachel stopped underneath the tree. "Where's Polly?"

"Here I am," called a tinkling voice.

The girls looked up, and there was Polly perched on a branch above their heads, swinging her legs.

"Did you find your party bag?" asked Rachel.

Polly's shimmering wings drooped a little. "No," she sighed. "Where can it be?" Then she brightened. "But I know where your Frisbee is," she added, pointing downwards. "It's right in the middle of that bush."

"Thanks, Polly," said Kirsty. She and

Rachel began to push the leaves aside, but as they did so, Polly suddenly cried out in alarm.

"Girls, watch out! There's a goblin!"

Goblin Chase

There was a loud rustling of leaves as the goblin pushed his way out of the other side of the bush. He had Polly's bright blue party bag in one hand, and the Brownies' Frisbee in the other. Kirsty and Rachel emerged from the bush, just in time to catch a glimpse of him as he raced off.

"Hee-hee," the goblin chuckled gleefully. "A party bag for Jack Frost, and a Frisbee for me. Hurrah!"

"Come back, you horrid goblin!" Polly called crossly. She zoomed after him, her wings fluttering so fast they were a shimmering blur. "Give me back my party bag!"

"After him, Rachel!" Kirsty cried, giving chase.

Polly, Kirsty and Rachel followed the goblin towards the stream.

"We've got him now, girls!" Polly declared triumphantly. "Goblins hate getting their feet wet."

But the goblin wasn't beaten yet.

Panting, he flipped the Frisbee over and launched it onto the water like a little boat. Then he grabbed one of the spoons the Brownies had used in the egg and spoon race and paddled away across the stream, looking very pleased with himself.

"Thought you'd caught me, didn't you?" he jeered, grinning all over his mean face. "Well, you haven't! Ha, ha, ha!" And he stuck his tongue out at the girls.

"We've got to stop him," Polly said anxiously. "It'll be easier if you two can fly, too." With a wave of her wand and a shower of sparkling fairy dust, Polly turned Kirsty and Rachel into fairies.

"Come on!" yelled Polly, as she skimmed out over the water like a beautiful blue dragonfly.

The goblin looked alarmed and began to row faster.

"How are we going to stop him?" Kirsty asked Rachel as they flew across the stream in pursuit.

"I don't know," Rachel replied,
looking round to see if there was
anything to help them.

All of a sudden,
Rachel spotted the
row of upturned
buckets which had
formed part of the
obstacle race. An idea
popped into her head, and she turned
and flew towards them. Meanwhile,
Polly was flying round the Frisbee-boat,

as close to the
goblin as
she dared,
trying
to snatch
her party
bag back.

"Get away from me!" the goblin howled furiously, paddling even harder.

"Not till you give me my party bag back!" Polly cried in a determined voice. She swooped down towards the goblin again, reaching out for the bag which lay in the bottom of the Frisbee. But, this time, the goblin lashed out with his paddle, and only just missed one of Polly's wings.

"Oh, Polly, be careful!" Kirsty called, wondering where Rachel had got to.

"Kirsty! Help me!"

Kirsty spun round to see Rachel
trying to pick up one of the obstacle
race buckets. As Rachel was now
fairy-sized, she was finding it difficult.
Kirsty fluttered over to help her.
"What's this for?" she asked,
helping Rachel lift the bucket.

"We need to get this over to the
goblin," Rachel panted.

Carrying the bucket between them,
the two girls flew over the stream.

The goblin had picked up the party bag now and was holding it tightly, jabbing at Polly with his spoon to keep her away.

"Turn the bucket upside-down, Kirsty," Rachel whispered, as they hovered above the goblin's head. "Ready? Now let go!"

Both girls let go of the bucket at exactly the same moment and it dropped right down over the goblin's head, covering him to his knees.

Polly's Sparkly Secret

"Great shot, girls!" Polly laughed. "Right on target!"

"Help!" the goblin yelled. He tried to knock the bucket off, but he couldn't because he was still holding his spoon-paddle in one hand and the party bag in the other. "Everything's gone dark!"

Moaning and groaning to himself, the goblin put the spoon and the party bag down in the bottom of the boat, and began trying to shift the bucket off with both arms. But Polly was ready for him. She swooped down and waved her wand over the goblin, showering

him with fairy dust. Immediately, the bucket stuck fast to his head. No matter how much the goblin twisted and turned, he couldn't shake it off.

"That's fixed you!" Polly declared happily.

But the goblin was still determined to get away. He began to paddle again, but because he couldn't see where he was going, he ended up drifting round and round in circles. Polly and the girls laughed.

"Stop laughing!" the goblin raged, banging the water crossly with his spoon-paddle. But Rachel flew over and took it away from him.

At the same time, Polly fluttered
down and picked up her party bag
from the bottom of the boat. "Thank
you so much, girls,"
she beamed,
hugging it close.
"No problem,"
Kirsty said. "But
what are we going to do
about him?" She pointed at
the goblin who was still moaning
to himself under the bucket.

"We'd better drag him and the
Frisbee to dry land," suggested Rachel.

Polly and the girls took hold of the
Frisbee and began towing the goblin
towards the bank.

"What are you doing?" the goblin
grumbled, "Where are you taking me?"

"You're coming back to Fairyland with me," Polly replied, clutching her party bag tightly."

"Don't want to go to Fairyland," the goblin muttered sulkily.

Rachel and Kirsty couldn't help laughing.

"Well, girls, you've saved the day again," Polly said, flying over to hug them both. "If the jubilee party is as much fun as I think it's going to be, it will all be thanks to you! And now I'd better get back to Fairyland." She raised her wand, but Kirsty gave a shout. "Wait, Polly!" she cried. "You've got to make Rachel and me human-sized again."

"Oops!" Polly laughed, "I almost forgot. You both make such good fairies!" She waved her wand, and a shower of glittering fairy dust swirled through the air and fell over both girls.

A few seconds later they were their
normal size again.

"Goodbye, Polly," Rachel smiled. "Say
hello to the other Party Fairies for us."

"And to everyone in Fairyland,"
added Kirsty.

But to their surprise, Polly was
hovering in mid-air, looking thoughtful.
"Before I go," she said, "there's just one
more thing I need to do…"

She opened her party bag, took out a handful of fairy dust and tossed it into the air. As the sparkling blue dust whirled and tumbled to the ground, Rachel and Kirsty were fascinated to see that it was all in the shape of tiny balloons.

"What are you doing, Polly?" asked Rachel curiously.

Polly grinned and waved her wand. As she and the goblin began to disappear in a shower of glittering fairy dust, she called, "You'll have to wait and see!" She winked at the girls. "For now, it's a secret!" and with that, she vanished.

A Touch of Magic

Kirsty and Rachel looked at each other in surprise, but at that moment they heard Mrs Talbot calling.

"Kirsty! Rachel! Where are you?"

Kirsty grabbed the Frisbee, and she and Rachel hurried back to join the other Brownies.

"Oh, there you are," said Mrs Talbot.

"You were a long time." She looked
down at the wet Frisbee. "Did it go in
the stream?"

"Yes, it took us a while to get it
back," Kirsty replied.

Rachel grinned. That was certainly
true, she thought.

"Well, have your juice and biscuits
quickly," Mrs Talbot went on. "We're
going to play another game now."

"Did you find the parcel for pass the parcel?" asked Emily.

Mrs Talbot looked a bit embarrassed and shook her head. "No, I didn't. I can't think where it's got to."

"I've found it," Mrs Carter said, walking towards them with a large parcel wrapped in glittering, multi-coloured paper. "It was on the mini-bus."

Mrs Talbot looked surprised. "That's not the parcel I..." she began doubtfully.

"Well, it must be," said Mrs Carter. "It's the only parcel here."

Rachel and Kirsty glanced at each other and smiled. Now they thought they knew what Polly had been up to when she took the fairy dust out of her party bag – this was a magic parcel from Polly the Party Fun Fairy!

"Come along, girls," called Mrs Carter. "Sit down on the grass in a big circle."

Kirsty and Rachel hurried to join their friends. Meanwhile, Mrs Talbot was still looking puzzled. "I don't remember using that sparkly wrapping paper at all!" she muttered to herself.

Mrs Carter handed the parcel to the nearest Brownie. "Now remember, girls, whoever's holding the parcel when the music stops gets to take off a layer of wrapping-paper."

"I can't wait to see what's inside," Kirsty whispered to Rachel, as Mrs Carter switched on the CD-player. The Brownies passed the large parcel round the circle until Mrs Talbot stopped the music. When she did so, Jenny was holding the parcel.

All the Brownies, including Rachel
and Kirsty, leaned forward eagerly as
she ripped the first layer of paper off.

"Oh!" everyone gasped.
Hundreds of clear,
shining bubbles
were floating
up into the
air, filling the
sky overhead
with rainbows.
Rachel and
Kirsty grinned
and nudged
one another.
"Look at Mrs
Talbot's face," Kirsty
whispered, chuckling.
"She can hardly believe her eyes!"

"I'm sure this can't be the parcel I wrapped..." Mrs Talbot was saying, but no one was taking any notice. They were too eager to see what other wonderful surprises the parcel contained.

Mrs Carter started the music again. This time, when it stopped and a Brownie removed a layer of wrapping, hundreds of pieces of glittering confetti burst out of the paper and floated down onto the grass, disappearing as they landed.

Next, the parcel
stopped with a
Brownie sitting
near Kirsty. She
tore a layer of
paper off, and
everyone gasped
as coloured sparkles
shot up into the air, then
burst overhead like tiny fireworks,
filling the sky with dazzling colours.

Just when the girls thought there
couldn't be any more surprises left, the
music stopped again while Rachel was
holding the parcel. Taking a deep breath,
she pulled the shiny piece of paper apart.

It was the last layer. A huge heap
of sweets, wrapped in colourful twists
of paper, spilled out onto the grass.

The Brownies cheered.

"Thank you, Polly," Rachel whispered to herself, as she and Kirsty began to hand the sweets out to the other Brownies.

"We've helped our fairy friends again, and we've had fun, too," Kirsty said, smiling at Rachel. She sighed happily. "Fairy adventures are always the best!"

Now it's time for Kirsty and Rachel to help...

Phoebe the Fashion Fairy

Read on for a sneak peek...

Kirsty Tate and Rachel Walker were busy wrapping a birthday present for Kirsty's friend, Charlotte.

"There," said Kirsty, tying the ribbon. "Charlotte's going to love this silver hairband, it's so pretty."

"Are you nearly ready, girls?" Mrs Tate called up the stairs.

"Dad and I have to leave in two minutes!"

"Just coming, Mum," Kirsty replied. Then she turned to Rachel. "I can't believe we're going to another party, can you?" she grinned.

Rachel shook her head. "I wonder what's going to happen this time," she said excitedly.

The two girls shared a secret. They were friends with the fairies! And while Rachel had been staying with Kirsty's family, the girls had been helping the Party Fairies of Fairyland. Grumpy Jack Frost had sent his goblin servants into the world to cause trouble at human parties. When a Party Fairy arrived to put things right, a goblin would try to steal her magical party bag and take it back to Jack Frost. Rachel and Kirsty had been helping the fairies keep their party bags safe – which meant that all the parties that week had been extra-specially exciting.

Kirsty and Rachel put their party dresses into a bag with Charlotte's present, then rushed downstairs.

Kirsty's parents had to go out that afternoon, so Mrs Tate had arranged for the girls to go to Charlotte's house a little early.

"We've met nearly all the Party Fairies now," Kirsty said, as she and Rachel walked along the road.

Rachel counted them off on her fingers. "Cherry the Cake Fairy, Melodie the Music Fairy, Grace the Glitter Fairy, Honey the Sweet Fairy and Polly the Party Fun Fairy," she said. "So the only two we haven't met are…"

Read Phoebe the Fashion Fairy to find out what adventures are in store for Kirsty and Rachel!

Meet the Party Fairies

Cherry the Cake Fairy

Melodie the Music Fairy

Grace the Glitter Fairy

Honey the Sweet Fairy

Polly the Party Fun Fairy

Phoebe the Fashion Fairy

Jasmine the Present Fairy

When Jack Frost steals the Party Fairies' magical bags, Kirsty and Rachel must come to the rescue before parties everywhere fizzle into flops!

www.rainbowmagicbooks.co.uk

Calling all parents, carers and teachers!
The Rainbow Magic fairies are here to help
your child enter the magical world of reading.
Whatever reading stage they are at, there's
a Rainbow Magic book for everyone!
Here is Lydia the Reading Fairy's guide to
supporting your child's journey at all levels.